The Ba

DATE DUE

**The galaxy is yours.
Be a part of**

STAR
WARS®
EPISODE I
ADVENTURES

**#1 Search for the Lost Jedi
#2 The Bartokk Assassins
#3 The Fury of Darth Maul**

. . . and more to come!

#2

STAR WARS®

E P I S O D E I

ADVENTURES
GAME BOOK

BY

The Bartokk Assassins

Ryder Windham

SCHOLASTIC INC.

New York Toronto London Auckland Sydney
Mexico City New Delhi Hong Kong

ISBN 0-439-10139-5

12 11 10 9 8 7 6 5 4 3 2 1   9/9 0 1 2 3 4/0

Printed in the U.S.A.
First Scholastic printing, October 1999

INTRODUCTION

Before the events of the Trade Federation's invasion of Naboo, the Jedi Council received a mysterious data card that alerted them to the construction of fifty droid starfighters, each equipped with hyperdrive engines. The Council sent Jedi Master Adi Gallia to the planet Esseles in the Darpa Sector to investigate. When Master Adi failed to report back from her mission, the Council sent a rescue team to Esseles.

Jedi Master Qui-Gon Jinn led the team that included two Jedi Knights: Vel Ardox, an amphibian from the Ploo Sector; and Noro Zak, a winged Baxthrax. Against the wishes of Mace Windu, Qui-Gon also brought his Padawan apprentice, Obi-Wan Kenobi.

On Esseles, the Jedi realized Adi Gallia was trapped within a starship factory that had been seized by renegade droids. After the Jedi rescued the factory's owner, a reptilelike Kloodavian named Boll Trinkatta, they learned the starfighters had been manufactured for the Trade Federation.

Trinkatta claimed he had not wanted to work for the Trade Federation, but he'd changed his mind after his test pilot had vanished. Trinkatta believed the Trade Federation was responsible for the pilot's disappearance, and feared for his own safety. The Kloodavian ordered his droids to build the starfighters.

Before the finished starfighters could be delivered to the Trade Federation, Trinkatta's droids were reprogrammed by the Bartokks, a species of insectoid mercenaries with a hive mind. The Bartokks had intended to use the droids to take over the starship factory and steal the droid starfighters. Much to the dismay of the Bartokks, the starfighters had already been stolen from Trinkatta's factory by an unknown enemy.

The Jedi defeated the reprogrammed droids along with two Bartokks, and Master Adi was found in need of medical treatment. Qui-Gon decided that Vel Ardox and Noro Zak would immediately escort Master Adi to the nearby planet Rhinnal, famed throughout the sector for its citizens' expertise in medicine.

Meanwhile, Qui-Gon and Obi-Wan remained on Esseles, where they hoped to track the trail of the stolen droid starfighters. Qui-Gon and Obi-Wan feared that the starfighters might have fallen into the clutches of someone even more menacing than the Bartokks or the Trade Federation. In need of a guide to Esseles' capital city Calamar, the Jedi enlisted the reluctant Trinkatta.

CHAPTER ONE

Qui-Gon Jinn belted himself into the front passenger seat of the landspeeder while Obi-Wan Kenobi slid behind the controls. Obi-Wan gunned the turbine engines and angled the speeder away from Trinkatta's starship factory and toward Calamar. The capital city was already visible in the distance, a silhouette of several hundred towers that hugged the lush, green horizon.

"This is madness!" Boll Trinkatta exclaimed from the speeder's backseat. "Even if all fifty droid starfighters are still on Esseles, how do you two hope to take them from the Bartokks?"

While the speeder zoomed over the grassy plains, Qui-Gon turned to his outraged passenger. "As I said, Trinkatta, the Bartokks don't have the starfighters. If they did, they wouldn't have left two assassins to guard your factory. With those two dead, the surviving thirteen members of the Bartokk hive are probably still searching for the ships."

"Then I should flee this planet immediately!" Trinkatta shouted, his beak opening wide. "And not just because I'm afraid of what the Bartokks might do to me. Since the droid starfighters weren't delivered to the Trade Federation, the Neimoidians who ordered them are probably already on their way to Esseles to investigate. They'll kill me if I can't deliver those ships."

"Then maybe you shouldn't have done business with the Trade Federation in the first place," Obi-Wan commented as he neatly directed the landspeeder over a dirt road that led into the city.

"I didn't have a choice," Trinkatta insisted. "If I hadn't built those starfighters, the Trade Federation would have made me vanish without a trace, just like my test pilot. I'm *lucky* those Bartokks only reprogrammed my droids to cut off one of my arms." Trinkatta winced at the memory of the violent interrogation. With his left hand, the reptile-like alien massaged his right elbow, where his lower arm was rapidly growing back.

As the landspeeder approached Calamar, Obi-Wan kept his eyes on the road. "Master! I don't understand why you suspect the droid starfighters are in Calamar. Wouldn't it have been smarter for someone to hide them at a remote location or even offworld?"

"Don't underestimate the intelligence of the thieves, Obi-Wan," Qui-Gon stated. "If they could steal fifty starfighters from Trinkatta's factory without alerting the Bartokks, they're very smart indeed. And in my experience, the best place to hide a needle is among other needles. I've a hunch the starfighters are in a spaceport."

"I don't believe it!" Trinkatta snapped. "You're risking my life over a hunch?"

Qui-Gon cast a sympathetic glance at the Kloodavian and replied, "Be assured, Trinkatta, no harm will come to you while you're with us. All we ask for is your help."

"But what can I do?" Trinkatta answered, shrugging his shoulders.

Qui-Gon raised an eyebrow at the alien. "You can start by telling us about your contact with the Trade Federation. Did Neimoidian leaders come to your factory?"

The Kloodavian nodded. "Yes, there were two of them. Officers, I think, although they never identified themselves. They brought a prototype hyperdrive engine with them and insisted I duplicate it for all fifty droid starfighters."

"And what about your test pilot?"

"He was a Talz named Bama Vook," Trinkatta replied. "He was an excellent pilot, even if he was sometimes a bit reckless. His copilot was an LE-PR34 navigator droid called Leeper. They were such good friends the droid didn't even address Bama as 'Master.' Oh, and Bama had a young son named Chup-Chup, a real rascal. The poor lad must be an orphan now. But why do you want to know about Bama? Like I said, the Neimoidans got rid of him."

"Actually, you said he *vanished without a trace*," Qui-Gon corrected. "Perhaps Bama Vook escaped from the Neimoidians, but they simply let you be-

lieve they were responsible. I can't help but wonder if Bama Vook's disappearance is somehow connected with the missing starfighters."

Obi-Wan shot a quick glance at Qui-Gon, then turned his attention back to the road. "Master, are you suggesting that Bama Vook is still alive, and that he stole the droid starfighters from Trinkatta's factory?"

"I'm not suggesting anything," Qui-Gon replied, then fixed his gaze on the Kloodavian. "Did Bama Vook ever mention that he had any friends in Calamar?"

Trinkatta scratched his head with his good hand while he tried to remember. "Now that I think of it, Bama *did* spend some time at a place over by Calamar Intergalactic Spaceport, a saloon that was popular with starpilots. It's called the Ion Sandbox."

"Then that's where we're going," Qui-Gon commanded.

When the air traffic controllers at Calamar Intergalactic Spaceport authorized the landing of a sleek, dark green starcruiser, they did not notice anything unusual about the vessel. The cruiser's identification numbers and three-winged profile matched those of an executive trade ship from the Duro system. The cruiser's two passengers had large eyes and thin slits for mouths. They did not have noses.

They were all physical attributes of the Duros species. The only problem was that the passengers were not Duros.

They were Neimoidians.

Disguised as Duros traders, Rune Haako and Daultay Dofine wore heavy green cloaks with tapered hoods. They exited their green cruiser and walked down the landing ramp to the gritty tarmac.

"I never thought we'd have to return to this dull planet," Haako muttered. "When I get my hands on Trinkatta, I'll crush his windpipe."

Dofine stopped and turned to his superior. "Are you sure we shouldn't transmit a message to Viceroy Gunray and let him know we've arrived on Esseles?" Dofine asked.

Lieutenant Haako's smooth brow furrowed. "Don't be a fool, Dofine! Have you forgotten this is a secret mission? Our orders were clear. We're to investigate Trinkatta Starships and learn why the droid starfighters were not delivered to us. Also, whoever informed the Jedi Council of the starfighters must be found and silenced."

"It was probably Trinkatta who alerted the Council," Dofine suggested.

"The Kloodavian wouldn't have had the nerve," Haako sneered. "After his test pilot disappeared,

Trinkatta knew better than to toy with the Trade Federation."

As the pair entered a lift tube to leave the hangar, Dofine dared to ask another question. "How do you think the Jedi Council have responded to the report of droid starfighters on Esseles, sir? I hope we do not encounter any Jedi."

As the lift tube came to a stop, Haako replied, "I doubt the Republic would send their precious Jedi to this horribly distant world."

The lift tube doors hissed open, and the disguised Neimoidians stepped outside. It was the end of the business day, and the streets of Calamar were filled with pedestrians and vehicles. The citizens of Calamar paid little attention to the two hooded aliens that walked away from the hangar entrance.

"We'll hire a landspeeder and approach Trinkatta's factory with caution," Haako declared. "If he's up to something, I want to catch him by surprise. But before we go, I need a little refreshment."

Daultay Dofine silently followed Lieutenant Haako into a nearby saloon. Over the entrance, the establishment's name was prominently displayed on a glowing sign: ION SANDBOX.

The Ion Sandbox resembled any number of spacer bars throughout the system. Aliens from all over and beyond the Bormea and Darpa Sectors swapped stories and rubbed elbows at the cramped tables. Instead of a live band, a holographic quintet shimmered and gyrated on a small elevated stage, their prerecorded performance dominated by thundering drums and blaring horns. Customers shouted their conversations over the music, and the air was filled with heavy smoke.

As the disguised Neimoidians stepped up to the bar, Dofine noticed a furry Talz seated at a corner table. One of the Talz's four eyes was covered by a black patch. Dofine nudged Haako and whispered, "That Talz over there looks a lot like Trinkatta's pilot."

"Don't be ridiculous," Haako replied. "Bama Vook didn't wear an eye patch."

As the Neimoidians ordered drinks, the tall Talz slowly rose from his corner table and headed for the back door.

CHAPTER TWO

Obi-Wan Kenobi guided the landspeeder through a narrow alley and parked next to the receptacles behind the Ion Sandbox. As soon as Obi-Wan turned off the speeder's loud engine, the noise was replaced by the sound of bizarre music and alien laughter that drifted out from the saloon.

Trinkatta jumped out of the speeder and adjusted his cape to cover both his head and injured arm. He didn't want anyone to recognize him. "Come quick," he urged Obi-Wan and Qui-Gon. "We'll enter through the back door."

The two Jedi climbed out of the speeder and followed the Kloodavian to a high oval doorway. Trinkatta was just about to step over the threshold when he bounced off a tall alien who was exiting the saloon. "Oof!" Trinkatta expelled as he hit the ground. When he looked up, he saw that the alien was a Talz. Trinkatta's jaw dropped open in surprise.

The Talz was covered in thick white fur and stood just under two meters tall. Around his neck, a collar was equipped with an expensive vocabulator that could translate his own guttural language into Basic. At his right hip, a heavy blaster was holstered to his weapons belt. His most distinguishing accoutrement was a black patch over his upper left eye.

"You don't fool me with that eyepatch, Bama!" Trinkatta snarled as he pushed himself up from the ground. "How dare you let me think the Trade Federation killed you!"

"You must have confused me with someone else, stranger," Bama Vook replied via his vocabulator. Then he leaned forward so his nose nearly touched the Kloodavian's, and raised the black patch to reveal a perfectly healthy eye, which he winked at Trinkatta. In a low voice, Bama said, "Yes, it's I, Trinkatta, but keep your infernal voice down. There are two Neimoidians inside the bar. They're the same pair that threatened me at your factory."

Bama Vook rose to his full height and readjusted his eyepatch. "Sorry about pulling a vanishing act on you, Trinkatta, but I didn't want to wind up working for the Trade Federation. The owner of the Ion Sandbox owed me a favor, so he let me hide out here. You could have blown my cover, blundering into the bar with these two humans."

Trinkatta nodded to Qui-Gon, allowing the Jedi Master to make his own introduction. "I'm Qui-Gon Jinn and this is Obi-Wan Kenobi. The Jedi Council sent us. You must be the one who sent the data card that alerted the Council to the droid starfighters."

"You're Jedi?" Bama asked with disbelief, but something in Qui-Gon's expression convinced him otherwise. "Thank the stars, you came to help! Yes, I sent the data card."

Obi-Wan was stunned by this latest revelation. "Excuse me, Master, but how and when did you figure out that Bama sent the data card?"

"As soon as I realized Bama Vook was still alive, it all added up," Qui-Gon answered. "Since Trinkatta didn't send the data card, I surmised Bama must have done it after he escaped the Neimoidians."

"Indeed, that's exactly what I did," Bama beamed. "As soon as those two Neimoidians arrived at Trinkatta's factory, I knew the Trade Federation was up to no good. It's bad enough they're operating outside their own territory, but it's worse that they commissioned droid starfighters with hyperdrive engines. With those ships, they could level most of Calamar! Well, I wasn't about to let that happen."

Qui-Gon smiled at Bama. "Your experience as a pilot for Trinkatta Starships must have made it easy for you to liberate the droid starfighters from the factory." Qui-Gon's statement amazed Obi-Wan, who felt as if he were always three steps behind his Master's deductions.

"It was hardly easy," Bama confessed. "I kept my eye on the factory from a distance. At first, I was trying to figure out a way to break in and destroy the starfighters. But two nights ago, I saw someone loading the starfighters into a spike-covered freighter. I figured they were working with the

Neimoidians. While my copilot Leeper distracted them, I bypassed Trinkatta's security system, broke into the factory, and stole the freighter. I thought it would be best to hide the ships until the Jedi Council could investigate the Neimoidians."

Trinkatta was stunned. "You *admit* you stole the starfighters?" he cried.

"I got more than that," Bama said with pride. "The freighter also contained the Neimoidians' prototype hyperdrive engine. Without that prototype, they'll have a tough time building any more droid starfighters on Esseles."

Trinkatta fumed. With his left arm, he pushed back his cape to reveal his injured arm. "Forgive me, Bama, if I don't applaud!"

Seeing Trinkatta's mangled limb, Bama gasped and his four eyes went wide. "The Neimoidians cut off your arm?"

"No, it was my droids." Trinkatta sighed as he readjusted his cape. "They were reprogrammed by Bartokks who were trying to steal the starfighters, but you'd already beaten them to the job. You stole the Bartokks' freighter, you imbecile!"

"Bartokks?" Bama exclaimed as his eyes rolled in their sockets. "Why are those assassins on Esseles?"

"We don't know for certain," Qui-Gon admitted. "But it's an easy guess the Bartokks are on an assignment to kill someone. We suspect they want the Trade Federation's droid starfighters and prototype hyperdrive engine to carry out their own plan. We're wasting time here. Where did you store the freighter?"

"In Docking Bay 28," Bama answered. "That's where I keep my own ship, the *Metron Burner.* Leeper and my son, Chup-Chup, are guarding the freighter now. I only came to the Ion Sandbox to find out if there were any reports of Republic ships in the area. I never imagined the Jedi would get here so soon."

"With both the Bartokks and the Neimoidians on Esseles, I hope our arrival isn't too late," Qui-Gon said. "Our landspeeder's right here. Will you guide us to Docking Bay 28, Bama?"

"Gladly!" Bama answered with enthusiasm.

"I still can't believe you broke through my security system," Trinkatta grumbled to Bama as they climbed into the speeder.

Back in the saloon, Rune Haako lowered his empty glass onto the bar. "We're done here," Haako announced, "Come along, Dofine. Time to pay a visit to Trinkatta Starships."

The two cloaked Neimoidians made their way out of the Ion Sandbox and onto the street. "Now, find us a taxi," Haako ordered as he pulled his cloak lower over his forehead.

Dofine heard the roar of a landspeeder engine

and turned just in time to see the vehicle launch out of a nearby alley. Dofine raised his hand and was about to call out to the speeder's driver — a young male Human — when he recognized Trinkatta and Bama Vook as the passengers in the backseat. An older male Human sat beside the driver.

Dofine's arm dropped to his side as the speeder zoomed down the street. He turned to Haako and said, "Sir? I think we have trouble. I just saw Trinkatta and Bama Vook in a landspeeder. They were with two humans."

"What?" Haako snapped. "Which way did they go?"

Dofine pointed down the street, where the speeder was still barely visible.

"Well, don't just stand there," Haako commanded. "Start running!"

CHAPTER THREE

Docking Bays 25–30 were not far from the Ion Sandbox, and the Jedi's landspeeder made the short journey in less than three minutes. Each docking bay was a four-story structure that resembled a giant tire lying on its side; the circular architecture wrapped around and protected the sunken bay from view, but the open central area allowed immediate access for launches and landings. The streets that bordered the docking bays resembled a series of interlocking roundabouts.

"The docking bays are larger than I imagined," Qui-Gon commented. "But then they'd have to be large to accommodate a Bartokk freighter." Turning his head slightly, he addressed Bama Vook. "You mentioned your own ship, the *Metron Burner.* What's its make and model?"

"The *Metron Burner* is a Corellian YT-1300 Transport," Bama replied via his vocabulator.

"The latest model?" Obi-Wan asked with some disbelief. Obi-Wan knew the sizable YT-1300 freighters were fairly expensive.

"Not the latest, but still in good shape," Bama answered. "It was a good deal. Leeper, Chup-Chup, and I have also been remodeling a Z-95 Headhunter, making it suitable for space travel. We've expanded its cockpit to hold two pilots."

As Obi-Wan slowed the speeder near Docking Bay 28, Bama removed a comlink from his weapons belt. "Drive around to the north side,"

Bama instructed. "There's a lift tube just around this curve."

The lift tube was an industrial open-doored booth design built into the side of the ring-shaped structure. Obi-Wan slowed the speeder to a stop next to a stack of empty cargo containers. Across the street, in front of Docking Bay 27, a large chemical waste storage tank rested on a rusted gravsled outside.

"What a horrid stench," Bama said, pointing to the tank. "My neighbor better call a droid sanitation crew to tow that gravsled or I'll report him to the authorities."

The street was strangely silent and absent of any traffic. As Qui-Gon, Obi-Wan, Bama, and Trinkatta climbed out of the speeder, both Jedi cast cautious glances at the surrounding buildings.

"Something wrong?" Trinkatta asked.

Without any elaboration, Qui-Gon replied, "A disturbance in the Force."

On Docking Bay 27's roof, a quick movement and flash of insectoid armor caught Obi-Wan's attention. "Bartokks!" he said. He turned to Trinkatta and Bama. "They're above us. Take cover."

Trinkatta followed the Jedi's gaze. "I don't see anyone up —" he began. Before the Kloodavian could complete his sentence, Qui-Gon's arm lashed out and yanked him aside. A split-second later, a long, sharp spear flew down from above and plunged deep into the ground where Trinkatta had just been standing.

Qui-Gon shoved Trinkatta under the parked landspeeder and ordered, "Keep out of sight!" Three more spears raced down through the air, all aimed at the Jedi Master. Qui-Gon moved so fast he became a barely visible blur. As the spears drove into the ground, Qui-Gon rematerialized against the wall to the right of the lift tube booth. From this position, he was just out of the Bartokks' range of fire. On the other side of the booth, Obi-Wan and Bama ducked behind the stack of empty cargo crates.

"Judging from those spears, there are at least three Bartokks up there," Obi-Wan observed.

"How did they find us!?" Trinkatta yelped.

"Bartokks communicate telepathically," Qui-Gon replied as he scanned the rooflines for any sign of movement. "Before the two Bartokks were killed at your factory, they might have mentally transmitted a warning to the other thirteen members of their hive, alerting them to our presence on Esseles."

"Then it's possible we led them right here to Docking Bay 28," Obi-Wan realized with some frustration.

A pneumatic hiss indicated the lift was rising within the tube. As the lift reached the street level, the hiss ceased and a LE-PR navigator droid stumbled out through the booth's open doors. A nasty-looking dent was visible on the droid's metal forehead.

"Leeper!" Bama exclaimed. In a swift movement, Bama reached out and pulled the droid away from the booth and behind the empty cargo crates. Bama was barely behind the crate when a dozen poisoned-tipped arrows whizzed down from the roof. The arrows produced a rippling, staccato noise as they slammed into the wall near the booth, mere centimeters from Bama's head.

"What happened?" Bama asked the droid. "Where's Chup-Chup?"

"Sorry, Bama," Leeper answered in a deep synthetic voice. "Chup-Chup and I were watching the freighter when aliens jumped us. Insectoids with four arms. The freighter's owners, I suspect." The droid pointed to his dented forehead. "They took me by complete surprise. They pinned my arms and threw me into the lift tube before I could activate my blaster." Although it was an unauthorized modification, a retractable blaster was concealed within Leeper's right arm. "Just before the lift ascended, I saw them take Chup-Chup onto the freighter."

"What?" Bama gasped in disbelief. "Oh, I didn't mean to steal a Bartokk freighter!"

Twelve more arrows zinged down and struck deep into the protective cargo crate. Obi-Wan quickly studied the arrows' angle of impact. "Don't let the number of arrows fool you," he warned the Talz and the droid. "Each Bartokk is firing four arrows at a time."

Leeper glanced at Obi-Wan and Qui-Gon, then nudged Bama and asked, "Who are these guys?"

"We're Jedi," Qui-Gon informed the droid. "Tell us — is the Bartokks' freighter equipped with a hyperdrive engine?"

"No," Leeper replied. "I inspected the ship. Despite its cargo, the freighter itself only has a sublight engine. The Bartokks won't be making a fast getaway. Just wait until I get my manipulators on them!"

Another volley of arrows showered down around the heroes. Qui-Gon looked to Obi-Wan and said, "We must get past these snipers and board that freighter."

"Why not just destroy the freighter and all its contents?" Obi-Wan asked. Seeing Qui-Gon's reprimanding gaze and sensing Bama's outrage, Obi-Wan quickly added, "I mean, why not destroy it after we rescue Bama Vook's son?"

"Bartokks always have a backup plan in case something goes wrong," Qui-Gon informed his apprentice. "Destroying the freighter won't necessarily prevent another team of assassins from completing the Bartokks' assignment."

Obi-Wan considered Qui-Gon's assessment, then added, "If we can access the freighter's nav computer and learn the Bartokks' destination, we could figure out the identity of the Bartokks' target. Then we could warn the intended victim."

Qui-Gon nodded. "Now you're thinking, Padawan. We should also retrieve the Neimoidian prototype engine. The Council will want to have a look at —"

Before Qui-Gon could finish, three Bartokks sprang down from the roof of Docking Bay 27. Despite the weight of their gleaming black body armor, the assassins barely made a sound as they landed on the street.

Qui-Gon and Obi-Wan stood ready — but did not draw their lightsabers. The Bartokks waited, slightly hunched, braced on their segmented legs in an assault position. Each assassin wielded two twin-shaft crossbows, and they all aimed for Bama Vook's heart. Under the parked landspeeder, the cringing Kloodavian let out a gasp.

"Smart, you are, Jedi," the nearest Bartokk muttered in a digitized voice. Like Bama, the Bartokk wore a vocabulator that translated his native language into Basic. "Despite your speed, you know it is unlikely you could prevent all twelve arrows from reaching their mark. You will allow the freighter to leave Esseles, or the Talz and his hostage son will die."

"What assurance do we have that Bama's son is still alive?" Qui-Gon asked.

With one of his free arms, the Bartokk extended a comlink. He pressed a switch, and the frightened cry of the captured Chup-Chup was broadcast from the comlink's speaker.

With a flick of his claw, the Bartokk switched off the comm. "As you could hear, our hostage is still breathing."

Bama snarled as he reached for his holstered blaster, but Obi-Wan grabbed the Talz's wrist. "Careful," Obi-Wan whispered. "It's not just their arrows you should be worried about. The Bartokks' intelligence is distributed through nerve centers throughout their bodies. Even if you shoot off a head, the other parts of the body would continue to attack."

Suddenly, the nearly deafening roar of large repulsorlift engines filled the air. "That's the freighter!" Bama realized. "They're preparing for liftoff!"

Qui-Gon's voice was calm as he addressed the Bartokks. "You won't get away with this."

"What are you hotshots waiting for?" Trinkatta whimpered to the Jedi from beneath the landspeeder. "Do something!"

At this point, you must decide whether to continue reading this adventure, or to play your own adventure in the *The Bartokk Assassins* Game Book.

To play your own adventure, turn to the first page of the Game Book and follow the directions you find there.

To continue reading this Jedi adventure, turn the page!

CHAPTER FOUR

It's not the Talz's fault, Obi-Wan thought to himself. *If only Qui-Gon hadn't allied himself with such vulnerable riffraff.*

Cornered near the lift tube at Docking Bay 28, Obi-Wan was confounded by the present situation. Although he was confident that he and Qui-Gon could survive an encounter with the Bartokks, Obi-Wan wasn't so certain they'd be able to prevent the assassins from firing their arrows at Bama Vook.

From his position next to the cargo crates, Obi-Wan heard the rumble of the Bartokk freighter's engine within the docking bay. He didn't know much about Bartokk assassins, but he knew they did not have a reputation for letting hostages survive. He doubted the assassins had any intention of releasing Bama's son, Chup-Chup.

As Obi-Wan's eyes remained on the three assassins, his peripheral vision picked up a flickering movement: a shadow gliding across the outer wall of the docking bay across the street. The shadow was cast by something directly above him, and he looked up in time to see a wide stun net dropping from the roof. In that instant, Obi-Wan realized the three Bartokks on the ground were a mere distraction for a fourth assassin to spring a trap.

In the same instant, the young Padawan knew there wasn't any time to warn his Master, the Talz, or the droid. Obi-Wan's reflexes kicked in almost before he realized what he was doing. Faster than the eye could follow, he dove through the air and rolled under the landspeeder. His hand flew over Trinkatta's beak, preventing the Kloodavian from shouting in fright.

As soon as the stun net landed on Qui-Gon, Bama, and Leeper, it released a massive electric charge. The net's duracord strands glowed bright white-blue as the shock was unleashed. The Jedi Master and Talz were immediately knocked unconscious and the droid's circuits were shorted. The shock ended with a sick, fizzling sound. Trapped within the net, the three figures collapsed in a heap on the ground.

From under the landspeeder, Obi-Wan watched the three assassins on the street. He couldn't see the one on the roof, but it seemed the Bartokks had not witnessed his escape from the trap.

Obi-Wan waited to strike. He didn't enjoy the idea of harming any living creature, but he was more than prepared to give the ruthless Bartokks a fight they wouldn't soon forget. Trinkatta released a muffled groan, and Obi-Wan eased his hand from the Kloodavian's dry beak.

At the same time, the three Bartokks relaxed their grips on their crossbows and stepped closer to the stun net. Their movements were identical. With their hive mind, the insectoid creatures moved in the same fashion, like puppets controlled by a single brain.

Obi-Wan's mind raced. He wondered if the Bartokks realized yet that one of their targets had escaped the stun net. Would they leave for the freighter or search for him? Would he be able to board their freighter without anyone getting killed?

Before Obi-Wan could wonder anymore, each of the three Bartokks reached to his backpack and retrieved a spear. Then they raised the spears and prepared to bring the sharp points down on the defenseless bodies within the stun net.

Obi-Wan knew it was time to make his move.

The Padawan rolled fast out from under the landspeeder and came up with his lightsaber. His body blurred into invisibility as he surged toward the three Bartokks like a hostile wind. He activated the lightsaber. The Bartokks never saw him coming.

Obi-Wan materialized near the docking bay lift tube booth. His illuminated lightsaber was still clasped in his hands as he heard the sound of body parts hitting the ground. He had cut off the Bartokks' arms. All twelve of them.

If the Bartokks were in any way startled, they did not reveal it. While the emotionless assassins turned their bulbous-eyed heads to face Obi-Wan, their severed arms skittered on the ground, trying to pick up the fallen weapons.

Hoping to draw the Bartokks away from Qui-Gon and the others, Obi-Wan ran across the street and stood near a chemical waste storage container. Two of the armless Bartokks jumped at Obi-Wan. He dodged them, vanishing as they landed next to the storage container. As the Bartokks' arms skittered toward their respective bodies, Obi-Wan reappeared and drove his glowing blade through the container, then leaped aside to safety. The ruptured tank sprayed chemical waste onto the two Bartokks and their twitching limbs, effectively liquefying them in a toxic shower.

As the two Bartokks melted, Obi-Wan caught sight of their accomplice near the stun net. The surviving armless Bartokk raised a powerful leg, preparing to stomp the unconscious figures within the stun net. Obi-Wan again moved with incredible speed, and the Bartokk was suddenly minus both of its legs as well.

The Bartokk hissed and wobbled forward, moving like a massive, armored worm in an effort to use its mandibles to take a bite out of Obi-Wan. The Padawan raised a hand at the Bartokk and concentrated, using the Force to push the murderous monster back. The dismembered assassin slid quickly across the ground, leaving a slick trail in its wake until it reached its final destination in the chemical spill.

An ear-piercing shriek sounded from above. Obi-Wan glanced up in time to see a single Bartokk perched at the curved edge of Docking Bay 28's roof. Although all Bartokks were nearly identical, Obi-Wan was fairly certain it was the same Bartokk who threw the stun net. He imagined the Bartokk was furious for what had happened to the other assassins.

The Bartokk pulled a broad-bladed gutting knife from his weapons belt and sprang out into the air, descending headfirst toward Obi-Wan.

CHAPTER FIVE

Obi-Wan jumped aside, and the Bartokk reacted by coiling its insectoid body in midair. The assassin hit the ground in a perfect dive-forward roll and came up standing.

Before Obi-Wan could attack, the Bartokk's upper right arm snapped forward and aimed a crossbow at the figures in the stun net. With another claw, the Bartokk motioned for Obi-Wan to drop his lightsaber.

The Padawan knew if he were to deactivate his lightsaber and drop it on the ground, the Bartokk would probably shoot at the net anyway. Impatient for Obi-Wan's response, the alien gnashed its mandibles and hissed.

Obi-Wan threw his lightsaber in a tight spiral at the loathsome assassin. The lightsaber's blade sliced through the Bartokk's right shoulder and severed the crossbow-wielding arm. As the arm struck the ground, its claw tightened on the crossbow trigger and released two arrows directly into the assassin. The Bartokk's legs buckled, then the creature toppled face first onto the ground.

The spiraling lightsaber looped back through the air and returned toward Obi-Wan. The Padawan had used the Force to control his weapon's every move. He snatched the lightsaber from the air and thumbed the switch to deactivate its lethal blade.

Obi-Wan went to the fallen Bartokk and removed

the alien's vocabulator. Although he doubted the Bartokks would want to negotiate their surrender, Obi-Wan thought he might need the translating device to communicate with the assassins. On the Bartokk's weapon belt, Obi-Wan noticed what appeared to be a remote control unit for the stun net. He grabbed the control unit and ran to his unconscious allies.

Suddenly, the nearly deafening roar of a large repulsorlift engine filled the air again. Obi-Wan looked up and saw the spike-covered Bartokk freighter as it rose up and away from Docking Bay 28.

The Bartokk freighter was a massive vessel, nearly seventy meters long and twenty-five meters wide. To Obi-Wan, it resembled a bloated, barb-encrusted sea creature. Even the large, triangular sensor dish that jutted out from one side of the vessel seemed more like a fin than a technical extension. On the freighter's other side, a six-winged Bartokk starfighter was moored to the outer hull. Secured to the freighter, the starfighter looked like a mutant offspring clinging to its gargantuan mother.

Obi-Wan guessed that the Bartokks had delayed their liftoff in anticipation of an easy victory on Esseles. The freighter's sudden departure indicated they had given up this round.

It would take several minutes for the freighter to reach the upper stratosphere of Esseles and enter space. Although Qui-Gon might have criticized Obi-Wan for his decision, the Padawan took the time to free his unconscious friends from the stun net. He would give chase to the freighter as soon as possible.

The stun net no longer released any electric power, but its duracord strands were locked tightly around Qui-Gon, Bama, and Leeper. Obi-Wan examined the Bartokk-designed remote control unit, then pressed a switch to release the stun net.

The net glowed suddenly, and Obi-Wan quickly threw the switch off. He realized he had accidentally pressed the wrong switch and caused another shock to pass through Qui-Gon, Bama, and Leeper. Although it had been a mild shock and Qui-Gon and the others were already unconscious, Obi-Wan felt horrible for having caused them any more discomfort. Furthermore, they were still trapped within the net.

As Obi-Wan examined the remote control unit more carefully, Trinkatta slithered out from under the parked landspeeder. "Is it over?" asked the Kloodavian. "Are our friends all right?"

"They'll be fine," Obi-Wan answered, then added, "no thanks to you."

"What's that supposed to mean?!" Trinkatta snapped. "Can I help it if the sight of Bartokks scares the stuffing out of me?" Trinkatta leaned forward and looked at the Bartokk-designed device clasped by Obi-Wan. It had ten colored buttons. "What's this? A stun net remote control?"

"Don't worry," Obi-Wan said as he lowered a finger toward a green button on the device. "I think I've figured out how to use it."

With his good arm, Trinkatta lashed out and grabbed Obi-Wan's wrist. "First of all, you're holding the remote upside down," warned Trinkatta. "Second, that button you were about to push will kill everything within the net. Now, if you'll allow me?"

Obi-Wan handed the remote control unit over to Trinkatta, who pressed two yellow buttons at the same time. Instantly, the stun net fell away from the three unconscious bodies.

Trinkatta saw the look of concern in Obi-Wan's face as the Padawan pulled his Master's limp body up from the ground. "He'll be okay," the Kloodavian assured. "They'll all be fine. They just need some time to recover."

Obi-Wan carefully lifted Qui-Gon and carried him to the parked landspeeder. After Obi-Wan placed his Master within the vehicle, he turned for Bama Vook. "Help me with this guy, Trinkatta. He's pretty heavy."

Without argument, the Kloodavian helped carry both Bama and Leeper to the landspeeder. After the three unconscious figures were secured, Trinkatta asked, "So what's your plan, kid?"

"You should take this speeder back to your factory," Obi-Wan answered. "Until they wake up, our friends here need someone to watch over and protect them. They need *you*, Trinkatta."

"But . . . why can't you watch them?" Trinkatta asked nervously.

"That Bartokk freighter's carrying the Trade Federation's starfighters and hyperdrive engine. I'm going after it."

"By yourself?" Trinkatta gasped. "Is that a good idea?"

"It's the only idea I have," Obi-Wan admitted. "The Bartokks have a hostage, and right now I'm the only one who can pursue them. Unless the Bartokks did something to Bama's starships, there should be a Corellian freighter and a Z-95 Headhunter in Docking Bay 28. I'll take a ship to fly after the freighter."

"But think of the odds you'll be up against," Trinkatta warned. "Let's see, fifteen Bartokks to a hive, minus the first two at the factory, then the three who jumped us, and the one with the net . . ." He wagged the fingers on his left hand as he counted. "Why, there are still nine Bartokks left in this gang of assassins!"

"Then wish me luck," Obi-Wan said as he picked up Trinkatta and dropped him onto the speeder's driver seat. "Now get moving"

Trinkatta started the speeder. As he zoomed down the street with his three passengers, Obi-Wan noticed two hooded figures lurking across the street. He was not certain, but they looked like two Neimoidians, possibly the same pair that Bama had described earlier. Obi-Wan wondered whether the Neimoidians had overheard his conversation with Trinkatta about the freighter's cargo, but he did not have time to deal with them. He ran for the lift tube to Docking Bay 28.

Obi-Wan pressed a switch but the lift did not descend. Something was wrong with the lift mechanism.

The headstrong Padawan did not waste time with any thoughts of repairing the damaged lift. Instead, he reached for his lightsaber, activated the blade, and carved a neat hole in the lift's metal floor.

The ruined metal grating fell away, tumbling down until it crashed at the bottom of the tube. Obi-Wan jumped down through the hole he had created and caught the edge of the broken grating. Clinging to the bottom of the lift, he dangled in the air. He realized the drop to the floor was farther than he had expected.

A wall-mounted energy cable offered a solution.

Obi-Wan reached out and grabbed the cable. He quickly scrambled down the cable to the floor of the docking bay.

Just as Bama had claimed, there were two star-ships. Obi-Wan recognized the different models. The larger ship was a bulky Corellian YT-1300 Transport with a starboard-mounted cockpit. The smaller ship was a dart-shaped, twin-engined In-com Z-95 Headhunter. According to Bama, the Headhunter had been modified to carry a second passenger and was capable of space travel.

Although the YT-1300 had a greater carrying capacity, Obi-Wan did not expect to retrieve much from the Bartokk freighter. The modified Head-hunter offered enough room for both Bama's son and the Neimoidian prototype hyperdrive engine. Because Obi-Wan suspected the Head-hunter was probably much faster, he decided against the Corellian transport and went for the Headhunter. Obi-Wan preferred speed over bulk any day.

Obi-Wan raised the Headhunter's canopy and slipped into the cockpit's front seat. He scanned the instrument panel and found himself impressed by the many modifications made by Bama and Leeper. Most remarkable was the way they had ex-panded the cockpit interior to accommodate a second seat behind the cockpit. There was even a fairly sophisticated autopilot system.

Setting the controls on manual, Obi-Wan prepared for liftoff. He reached up and lowered the canopy, but as it locked into position, he heard an odd beeping noise.

It was a bomb.

CHAPTER SIX

There wasn't any doubt in Obi-Wan's mind that the bomb had been placed in the Headhunter by the Bartokks. Anyone else might have simply disabled the starship's engine to prevent it from launching. Rigging the ship to blow up and kill anyone on board was more the Bartokks' style.

Closing the transparisteel canopy had triggered the bomb's timer. The beeping timer was also indicative of the Bartokks' flair for booby traps. They didn't just want their victims to be blown to pieces; they wanted them to know they were about to die.

Fortunately, Obi-Wan had studied bomb disposal on Coruscant and knew what to do. He located the trigger-wire that ran down from the timer in the canopy and traced it to the bomb's location. It was directly under the seat. He reached down and let his fingers hover over the bomb, using the Force to trace the weapon's subtle contours.

The bomb was a canister-shaped proton grenade, and Obi-Wan was familiar with the design. He pressed the twist plunger release and the grenade was instantly disarmed.

Obi-Wan removed the deactivated proton grenade from under his seat and gave it a quick study, then he secured it to his own weapons belt. He had a feeling the explosive device would come in handy later on, and he could hardly wait to return it to the Bartokks.

He activated the Headhunter's repulsorlift. Dust kicked out from under the Headhunter as its engines fired, and Obi-Wan steered the fighter up and out of Docking Bay 28. He accelerated and zoomed away from Calamar. The Headhunter rocketed into the sky with great speed as Obi-Wan clenched his teeth and gripped the controls. Less than a minute later, the fighter had ascended through Esseles' atmosphere and entered space.

Obi-Wan gazed outside the cockpit canopy and searched for the Bartokk freighter, but he only saw a field of stars. Even without a hyperdrive engine, the freighter was already well beyond visual range of Esseles.

Among Bama's many modifications to the Headhunter was a powerful scan-mode sensor. Obi-Wan activated the unit and two distant blips appeared on the scanner grid. Uncertain of which blip represented the Bartokk freighter, the Padawan closed his eyes and reached out with the Force. From across space, he sensed a trail of fear leading directly to the nearest blip on the grid.

Obi-Wan was certain the trail was emanating from the young Talz hostage. Although he was reassured to know Bama's son was still alive, it disturbed him to know the youth was in such a frightened state. Because of Obi-Wan's upbringing among the Jedi, fear was not something he easily understood, but he felt sorry for Chup-Chup and was eager to rescue him from the Bartokks.

Obi-Wan opened his eyes and shook his head. "Perhaps some of Qui-Gon's compassion has been rubbing off on me after all," he muttered to himself.

He entered the nearest blip's coordinates into the Headhunter's nav computer and activated the drive system. The Headhunter's speed increased so rapidly that he found himself suddenly pressed back into his seat. He fought the pressure and reached for the acceleration compensator. After he quickly stabilized the artificial gravity within the starship, Obi-Wan wondered if the Headhunter's modifications held any more surprises.

Two minutes later, the Bartokk freighter came into view. The Bartokks had ignored spacer protocol and switched off their running lights; their freighter appeared as a dark blot against the vast starfield. Except for the distinctive silhouette of the triangular sensor dish, Obi-Wan almost mistook the freighter for a large meteor.

An alarm sounded and a red light flashed within the Headhunter's cockpit. Obi-Wan had accidentally flown within the Bartokk freighter's sensor range. The freighter's running lights suddenly illuminated.

The Bartokks knew the Headhunter had arrived.

CHAPTER SEVEN

As Obi-Wan pondered his next move, he saw a small engine flare at the side of the freighter. The flare was from the engine exhausts of the six-winged Bartokk fighter craft. The fighter broke away from the larger ship and swung out in a wide approach toward the Headhunter.

Obi-Wan had once seen a diagram of a Bartokk starfighter. If he remembered correctly, such a fighter required a crew of three: a pilot, a gunner, and a tailgunner. The three Bartokks would be positioned with their backs to one another, and each assassin had a view through a triangular viewport. Because the Bartokks communicated telepathically and shared a hive mind, they functioned as a single twelve-armed pilot.

The Bartokk fighter fired a proton torpedo. As the explosive warhead streaked toward the Headhunter, Obi-Wan tried to avoid a direct hit by banking hard and away from its path. But instead of exploding, the torpedo curved back and continued to pursue the Headhunter. Obi-Wan realized the torpedo had a built-in homing sensor, and decided to take a more evasive action against his attackers.

With the torpedo hot on the Headhunter's tail, Obi-Wan pulled back on the controls and navigated his fighter through an insanely tight loop. The Headhunter rolled out of the loop and onto a straight course for the Bartokk freighter.

The Bartokks must not have anticipated Obi-Wan's daring maneuver, for the proton torpedo suddenly veered out of the Headhunter's trail and soared away from the freighter. Its retreating flightpath confirmed Obi-Wan's suspicion that the torpedo had been equipped with a remote destruct mechanism as well as a homing sensor. When the torpedo was a safe distance from the Bartokk ships, it detonated in a wild explosion.

The Bartokk starfighter zoomed so close to the Headhunter that Obi-Wan could see the three assassins in the craft's cockpit. The Bartokks pulled their fighter back in a tight loop and circled back to attack from the rear.

Obi-Wan's hands flew over his controls to channel energy from his engines to his deflector shields. The Bartokk gunner fired, and a hail of crimson energy bolts spat out from the laser cannons mounted to each of the fighter's six wings.

The energy bolts hammered at the Headhunter's shields, and Obi-Wan's ship shuddered at the assault. He knew the shields wouldn't hold up much longer, so he threw the Headhunter hard to the left, then right, then down into an outside loop. The Bartokk starfighter tried to follow Obi-Wan's zigzag path. Their ship seemed to wobble at high speed.

As soon as Obi-Wan saw the six-winged starfighter waver, he seized his opportunity and hit the

Headhunter's intertial dampers. The Headhunter appeared to flip and roll, but it was a controlled maneuver that brought the Bartokk starfighter into Obi-Wan's sights.

He fired the Headhunter's laser cannons and drilled the Bartokk starfighter. The Bartokk tailgunner trained his cannons on the Headhunter and fired back. Obi-Wan felt his ship's shields buckle as he targeted the tailgunner's viewport and released a concussion missile.

The missile streaked away from the Headhunter and smashed through the Bartokk starfighter's cockpit, then detonated. The explosion sent starfighter fragments in all directions.

Obi-Wan angled back toward the Bartokk freighter. During his battle with the six-winged starfighter, the freighter had neared the edge of an asteroid belt. Many of the asteroids were relatively small chunks of planetary debris, but some were much larger than the Headhunter.

As Obi-Wan approached the spike-covered freighter, he saw a hatch open at the main cargo hold. From out of the hatch, three objects were released into space. At first, Obi-Wan thought the freighter was jettisoning a few long pieces of metal scrap. This wouldn't have surprised him, since unethical pilots routinely dumped their junk in space to lighten their load and increase speed. But when the released objects extended dartlike wings and began to move toward the Headhunter, Obi-Wan realized the Bartokks had deployed something far more hazardous than space junk.

The three objects were droid starfighters.

The droid starfighters had been clearly programmed to attack Obi-Wan's ship, and would do so without fear or remorse. The three fighters assumed a triangulated assault formation and zoomed in for the kill.

Obi-Wan knew his deflector shields would not hold for long against the three fighters. He yanked the controls to the side and aimed the Headhunter for the nearby asteroid belt.

With one droid starfighter leading their formation, all three fighters followed the Headhunter. The field of asteroids became increasingly dense and difficult to navigate, but Obi-Wan poured on the speed.

The lead droid starfighter fired, unleashing a steady stream of red energy bolts after Obi-Wan. The Headhunter's shields absorbed the blasts, but Obi-Wan saw a warning light flash on his console. His ship wouldn't be able to take much more.

Obi-Wan drove the Headhunter into a sickening dive toward a wide, gray asteroid. The droid starfighters pursued him without a trace of hesitation. When the gray asteroid was so close that it nearly filled Obi-Wan's range of vision, he pulled out of the dive. The trailing droid fighters broke away from the dive, but the lead fighter was not able to pull out in time. It smashed into the asteroid like a glass ornament striking a stone wall.

For a moment, Obi-Wan thought he had also managed to lose the other two droid starfighters. Then he saw them soaring after him. They were gaining fast when he saw two oblong meteoroids suspended close to one another in space.

Obi-Wan aimed his ship at the space between the meteoroids, as a hail of energy bolts pounded at his shields from behind. As Obi-Wan passed between the two meteoroids, he flared his engines and pulled back on the controls. The backdraft from his engines caused the meteoroids to rotate on their axes and draw closer to one another. The nearest droid fighter was about to fire again at the Headhunter when it was crushed between the converging meteoroids.

The remaining droid starfighter kept a safe distance behind Obi-Wan, and unleashed a barrage of firepower on the Headhunter's deflector shields. Obi-Wan flew fast and hard, but no matter what he did, he couldn't seem to shake the last fighter.

Outside and beyond the asteroid field, Obi-Wan caught sight of the Bartokk freighter. Right then, he remembered an important fact about droid starfighters: instead of having individual electronic brains, each starfighter responded to commands transmitted by a remote central droid control unit. In this case, the control unit was probably located somewhere within the Bartokk freighter.

Obi-Wan punched a series of commands into the Headhunter's communications system. If he could isolate the droid starfighter's operating frequency, he could jam its signal. And if he jammed the signal, the fighter would be defenseless.

Despite his efforts, Obi-Wan could not manage to find the starfighter's operating frequency. However, he did not abandon the idea of knocking out the fighter's signal. He just decided to execute the idea in a more destructive manner.

Obi-Wan steered the Headhunter out of the asteroid field and flew after the Bartokk freighter. It was a dangerous tactic, since he was now out in the open and no longer surrounded by the protective cover of so many meteoroids. The droid starfighter followed him out of the field and increased speed.

The Bartokk freighter's outer hull was protected by the long metal spikes that protruded from its hull. Each spike was capable of releasing concentrated charges of energy. As the Headhunter drew within firing range, several spikes began to glow, then ejected deadly green charges at Obi-Wan's ship.

Obi-Wan neatly evaded the explosive charges and fired his laser cannons at the Bartokk freighter's triangular sensor dish. The dish was heavily reinforced, but Obi-Wan kept his finger on the trigger until the entire sensor array ruptured and exploded.

Behind the Headhunter, the last droid starfighter was suddenly cut off from its controlling brain. Flying without any guidance, the starfighter maintained its high velocity as it headed straight for the freighter.

Obi-Wan wanted to board the freighter before it released any more starfighters, so he angled back toward the large ship. The Bartokks' deflector-shield generator was located within a small dome on top of their freighter. The ship's protective spikes began to glow, preparing to fire again at Obi-Wan, but as the out-of-control droid fighter raced closer, the freighter's defense system targeted the droid fighter instead. While the freighter's spikes hurled energy charges at the incoming fighter, Obi-Wan targeted the Bartokk ship's deflector-shield generator.

There were simultaneous explosions as both the Trade Federation droid fighter and Bartokk shield generator blew. The freighter's shields dropped and Obi-Wan raced for the docking port that had been previously occupied by the six-winged starfighter. Before the freighter's spikes could recharge, Obi-Wan had docked the Headhunter. He knew the Bartokks would not fire at his ship when it was directly linked to their own freighter.

He scrambled out of his ship and into the freighter's docking port tube. An eight-sided metal hatch was built within a thick plastoid frame at the end of the tube. Obi-Wan pushed against the hatch and found that it was locked.

Obi-Wan passed his hand over an illuminated control panel to open the hatch. Suddenly, he heard a hissing sound. He realized he must have activated an anti-intruder security system and triggered the release of poison gas into the docking port tube.

Obi-Wan drew his breather to his face with one hand while he activated his lightsaber with the other. With a quick twist, he jabbed the lightsaber through the hatch and carved a large O through the thick metal. He took a step back then threw all his weight against the hatch, knocking it clear out of its plastoid frame and into the next chamber.

A great whooshing sound burst from the docking port tube, and Obi-Wan felt the air whip by him as if he had suddenly been caught in a strong wind. An automatic safety feature had kicked in, and it suctioned the gas out of the docking tube and into space.

Obi-Wan removed his breather and returned it to

his belt. Then he deactivated his lightsaber, but kept the weapon within his grip.

Obi-Wan moved forward into the Bartokk freighter. He found himself in a dark corridor that ran the length of the ship. He looked to his left and right and tried to get his bearings. From ventilation slats in the metal floor, steam rose and created a damp, wispy haze that impaired his ability to see either end of the corridor. He guessed that the Bartokks' bulbous, insectoid eyes did not require much light to find their way around on the ship.

Besides the darkness, there was an unusual sense of quiet within the corridor. The only thing Obi-Wan could hear was the steady, mechanical hum of the sublight engines, a sound that emanated from the main engine room at the left end of the corridor.

Since Obi-Wan had breached the Bartokks' security system in the docking port tube, he knew they must have been aware of his presence on their freighter. He was considering where to begin his search for the captured Chup-Chup when he saw a shadowy figure move toward him from the engine room area. The figure was clinging to the corridor's ceiling. A flash of metal indicated the figure carried a sharp knife.

Obi-Wan heard the sound of a crossbow being cocked. A quick glance to his right revealed that a second figure was moving toward him. It crawled along the grilled floor from the other end of the corridor.

Obi-Wan realized he was trapped between two Bartokk assassins.

CHAPTER EIGHT

Obi-Wan activated his lightsaber and the weapon illuminated the dank corridor. The Bartokks pounced.

The Bartokk who jumped from the ceiling was the first to meet Obi-Wan's lightsaber. The glowing blade swung through the assassin. The second Bartokk fired its crossbow. Obi-Wan flung himself against the wall, narrowly avoiding instant death by two poison-tipped arrows that tore past him and embedded in the ceiling. Obi-Wan swung his lightsaber hard and defeated the second Bartokk.

By cutting down the two Bartokks, Obi-Wan's battle had only begun. Since the aliens' intelligence was distributed throughout their bodies, they continued to fight even after being cut in half. The two Bartokks had now been divided into four dismembered parts, all of which scurried across the corridor floor and prepared to attack again.

Obi-Wan reached up to the ceiling and retrieved the two poison-tipped arrows. With expert skill, he flung both arrows at two of the insectoid fragments that clawed at him from the floor. The arrows drove through the black-armored exoskeleton and the two body parts flinched sharply before dying.

As the two dismembered figures lurched forward on their hacked torsos and aimed their claws at Obi-Wan, he brought his lightsaber down again and again, reducing the assassins to an unsightly pile of parts too small to be threatening.

Obi-Wan stepped away from the bits that lay strewn across the corridor floor. Even though he was without fear, Obi-Wan could not help but feel some revulsion for the violence that had just taken place. He wondered how Qui-Gon would have handled the Bartokks, and if his Master would have been in any way disappointed with his use of the lightsaber against such fierce opponents.

Obi-Wan pushed the thoughts from his mind. No matter what anyone thought, the facts remained the same: Bama Vook's son had been taken hostage by the Bartokks, and Obi-Wan was the young Talz's only hope for rescue.

By Obi-Wan's own calculation, only four Bartokks remained in this hive. If the two assassins in the corridor had managed to telepathically alert their comrades of his location before they died, he would still have to deal with four very angry Bartokks.

As he prepared to exit the corridor, Obi-Wan nearly tripped over one of the assassins' weapons belts. By the glow of his lightsaber, he examined the items on the belt. He found a pistol that packed a stun net charge, and also a slaving collar control device.

Slaving collars were crude mechanisms used to make prisoners behave themselves. If a collar-wearing captive tried to escape, the collar would release an ugly shock. Obi-Wan knew that the control device could also be used to track a captive. If such a collar had been used on Chup-Chup, Obi-Wan now had the resource to locate him.

Obi-Wan switched on the device and aimed it up and down the corridor. According to the illuminated panel, a captive was indeed wearing a collar, and was located in the main cargo hold.

Obi-Wan pocketed the control device and secured the stun net pistol to his belt. He walked up the corridor and cautiously entered the main cargo hold. Although he could not immediately see Chup-Chup, the starships had at least located the Trade Federation droid starfighters.

Like cave-dwelling winged rodents, the droid starfighters dangled upside down from a rack secured to the ceiling. The fighters had their wings folded up in transport mode. Even at rest, the starfighters were a menacing sight to behold.

But the hold was hardly filled to capacity. A quick count confirmed there were only twenty-two droid starfighters in the hold. Because Obi-Wan had destroyed only three droid starfighters in combat, he wondered what had happened to the remaining twenty-five Federation fighters.

Searching for Chup-Chup, Obi-Wan edged around a corner to find the hold's docking port. A magnetic field filled the rectangular port and separated the hold from outer space. Obi-Wan remembered his view of the freighter from outside and realized the three droid starfighters must have been deployed through this transparent port.

A clanking sound caused Obi-Wan to turn to his left, and he quickly spied two Bartokks. Holding tools, they were working on what looked like the Neimoidian prototype hyperdrive engine. The engine was clamped in place to a worktable that was set near the hold's docking port. Since Obi-Wan had never actually seen the prototype engine, he was not certain that this was indeed it. But from the engine's size and design, he knew it was highly probable.

Seeing Obi-Wan out of the corners of their bulbous eyes, the two assassins turned their monstrous heads in his direction. They dropped their tools and reached for their crossbows.

Obi-Wan's alert mind kicked into high gear, and everything appeared to slow down. His eyes scanned the hold and he saw an opportunity to eliminate this pair without touching his lightsaber. He was relieved, since he had no desire to repeat the battle in the corridor that had resulted in such carnage.

As the two Bartokks raised their weapons, Obi-Wan found a handgrip on the wall while he set his concentration on a switch near the worktable. The switch controlled the magnetic field that protected the hold from the vacuum of space. Obi-Wan grabbed hold of the grip on the wall, held his breath, and reached out with the Force to throw the switch.

The magnetic field dropped and a massive wind blasted through the port. The two Bartokks and several tools were torn out of the hold and into space. As soon as they were outside of the ship, Obi-Wan used the Force to throw the switch back into place. The magnetic field instantly raised, and the hold's air pressure returned to normal.

Obi-Wan ran to examine the prototype engine that remained secured to the worktable. Fortunately, it was still intact.

A desperate pounding came from the starboard airlock on the other side of the cargo hold. The circular airlock hatch was built into the thick plastoid wall. Airlocks were used to help spacers reacclimate to different environments, but in the wrong hands, the pressurized cabin could also be a death chamber.

Obi-Wan ran to the airlock. He peered through a bubble-shaped transparisteel viewport that offered a distorted view of the pressurized cabin's interior.

He saw the Talz, weirdly magnified through the bubble-shaped viewport. The hair-covered alien appeared taller than Obi-Wan had envisioned. The young creature was gasping for air and hammering his hairy fists against the walls.

To the left of the airlock, a gauge indicated the sealed chamber was depressurizing. Obi-Wan knew he would have to do something fast or the Talz would die. However, he was reluctant to use any of his weapons to open the airlock because the sudden pressure change might accidentally kill the child.

There were ten buttons on the airlock control board. Obi-Wan was unfamiliar with the functions of each button, but he knew a button was the best option to open the airlock. Although he never would have admitted it to anyone, he wished he had Trinkatta's technical expertise.

Trinkatta! As soon as he thought of the Klooda-vian, Obi-Wan remembered how he had deacti-vated the Bartokk stun net by pressing two yellow buttons on the remote control device. That device also had ten buttons.

There were two yellow buttons on the airlock control board. Obi-Wan pressed them both at the same time.

Obi-Wan's hunch was correct. The airlock re-pressurized and the Talz appeared to breathe more easily. Then the hatch opened with a hissing sound, and the Talz stepped out of the cabin. He had to duck to avoid hitting his head on the hatch's frame.

Obi-Wan looked up at the hairy alien.

Chup-Chup was 2.2 meters tall.

CHAPTER NINE

At the sight of the hulking child, Obi-Wan nearly fell over backward. "You're taller than your father!" Obi-Wan exclaimed.

Chup-Chup shrugged and pointed to his slaving collar. Using the device he'd retrieved from one of the Bartokks, Obi-Wan pressed two yellow buttons and the slaving collar fell from the Talz's neck. Chup-Chup pointed again to his furry throat, and Obi-Wan realized the Talz was without a vocabulator.

Remembering the vocabulator he had taken from the Bartokk on Esseles, Obi-Wan drew the device from his pocket and handed it to Chup-Chup.

Chup-Chup held the vocabulator in front of his mouth. "Thanks for rescuing me, mister," he said in a high voice. "Are you a real Jedi Knight?"

"Practically," Obi-Wan replied, eyeing the Talz with some suspicion. "What happened to you? Did the pressure in the airlock make you grow?"

The Talz giggled. "No, I'm just tall for my age. Did my father come with you?"

"No, he . . ." Obi-Wan stopped short, reluctant to cause any more worry for Chup-Chup. "Your father is still on Esseles, and he's looking forward to seeing you. He let me pilot his Headhunter here."

"He *let* you fly the Z-95?!" Chup-Chup asked with disbelief. "Wow. He must like you a lot."

"Chup-Chup, please listen," Obi-Wan said, his voice suddenly very serious. "There are two Bartokk assassins still at large on this freighter, so we should leave this ship as soon as possible." Obi-Wan glanced at the Neimoidian prototype hyperdrive engine on the worktable, then back at the tall Talz. "I want to examine this prototype engine. Do you think you can carry it to the Headhunter?"

"Sure!" Chup-Chup answered. "I'm good at lifting stuff."

The Talz unclamped the cumbersome engine from the table and tucked it under one of his thick arms. Carrying the engine, Chup-Chup followed Obi-Wan through the cargo hold and past the twenty-two droid starfighters.

"I was under the impression this freighter was carrying fifty droid starfighters when it left Esseles," Obi-Wan commented.

"It *was* carrying fifty starfighters," Chup-Chup continued. "But when the freighter entered space, another Bartokk freighter was waiting for us. The Bartokks transferred twenty-five starfighters to the second freighter."

"Transferred?" Obi-Wan said. "Of course! That would have been the Bartokks' backup plan in case they were pursued from Esseles." Then Obi-Wan remembered the second blip that had appeared on his scanner grid when he left Esseles' orbit. He realized that particular blip must have been another Bartokk freighter. Although Obi-Wan had little respect for the Bartokks, he couldn't help but acknowledge their cunning.

Obi-Wan led the Talz out of the cargo hold and into the long, dark corridor. He returned to the octagonal docking port tube and helped Chup-Chup board the Headhunter.

"Stay in the ship and wait for me," Obi-Wan ordered. "I still have to find out this freighter's destination."

Obi-Wan left the docking port tube and walked up the corridor to the control room. Numerous lights glowed and winked in the dim, filthy chamber. Thick cables dangled like mechanical vines from the ceiling, and a thin layer of moss covered some of the instruments. There was not any sign of the surviving Bartokk crew. The freighter appeared to be running on autopilot.

Without warning, a Bartokk dropped down from the ceiling.

The Bartokk carried four sharp gutting knives. He came at Obi-Wan with immense speed and fury. Obi-Wan knew that if he hesitated, the Bartokk would open him up like a ripe blumfruit.

Obi-Wan drew the stun net pistol and fired. The net shot through the air and snagged on the assassin, slamming him back against a moldy console. The duracord webbing glowed and stunned the Bartokk, and he fell to the control room floor.

The battered Bartokk breathed in a harsh rasp. His insectoid body slumped against the console that housed the freighter's nav computer. Obi-Wan noticed that the Bartokk wore a vocabulator.

"What were you planning to do with the starfighters?" Obi-Wan asked.

The Bartokk remained silent.

"What's your destination?" Obi-Wan asked, using the Force to apply pressure to the assassin.

The Bartokk squirmed. Obi-Wan concentrated hard, trying to search the alien's mind. But the Bartokk's intelligence was maddeningly intricate, with trillions of nerve cells thinking of nothing but murder.

"Corulag," gasped the Bartokk before he realized he had actually spoken out loud.

"What?" Obi-Wan said. "Who were you planning to kill on Corulag?"

"You will not defeat the Bartokks," the angry assassin hissed through his mandibles. "Our assignment will be carried out no matter what!"

"I already know about the transferred droid starfighters," Obi-Wan revealed. "I'll make sure the freighter never reaches its destination. Just wait until I turn you over to the authorities."

"I would sooner die than remain your hostage!" the Bartokk sneered. Suddenly, he twisted his neck sharply and bit down. His mandible contained a quick-acting toxin. Before Obi-Wan could intervene, the Bartokk was dead.

Obi-Wan quickly consulted the nav computer. The records showed the freighter was indeed set on a course for the planet Corulag. Obi-Wan realized the Bartokk freighter probably contained too many booby traps to reprogram a new destination or allow its return to Esseles. To prevent the freighter and its cargo of droid starfighters from reaching Corulag, Obi-Wan decided to destroy the entire ship.

Obi-Wan removed the proton grenade from his weapons belt. It was the same grenade the Bartokks had planted under the seat in the Headhunter. Obi-Wan knew that if the grenade were set in the control room, it would cause a chain reaction and blow up the freighter.

He set the timer for a two-minute countdown, then twisted the grenade's arming mechanism. This action primed the grenade's battery to deliver a small electrical charge to the proton core. Obi-Wan pressed the activation plunger to start the timer, then secured the grenade under the nav computer.

Obi-Wan ran from the control room and raced down the dark corridor. His feet pounded on the metal floor and the rising steam whipped at his face. He was almost at the octagonal docking port when he saw a dark form slip out from the shadows.

It was the last Bartokk assassin. Each one of his four arms wielded a different weapon: a gutting knife, a spear, a crossbow loaded with two poison-tipped arrows, and a stun net. Unexpectedly, he dropped all the weapons and let them fall to the corridor floor. At first, Obi-Wan thought the Bartokk was offering his surrender, but something in the alien's inviting stance conveyed that he had something else in mind.

The Bartokk wanted to take Obi-Wan apart with his own bare claws.

The corridor was still thick with the smell of death from Obi-Wan's earlier encounter with two Bartokks. He knew that it was not so easy to use a lightsaber against a Bartokk in such close quarters. He took a cautious step toward the docking port tube.

The Bartokk lashed out and tore through his opponent's tunic. Obi-Wan decided to take his chances with the lightsaber. His weapon blazed and he whipped the blade back and forth at his relentless attacker. Soon, there were over a dozen dismembered insectoid body parts clawing at the Jedi apprentice.

Obi-Wan kicked at the severed limbs that continued to crawl after him into the docking port tube. Chup-Chup was already seated in the back of the Headhunter. Obi-Wan jumped into the front seat and dropped the canopy.

"Why didn't you start the Headhunter's engine?" Obi-Wan asked, trying to keep his voice calm. "The freighter's going to explode in less than thirty seconds."

"But you didn't ask me to start the engine," Chup-Chup whimpered. "Besides, I'm not old enough to fly a starship."

"Then hang on!" Obi-Wan commanded. He punched the controls and the engines roared to life. The Headhunter broke off from the freighter and blasted away.

Within the Bartokk freighter, the proton grenade detonated just as the Headhunter began to fly off. Suddenly, the entire freighter erupted in a violent explosion that sent a small shock wave across space.

"Where to now?" Chup-Chup asked from behind Obi-Wan's seat. "We're not going after the other Bartokk freighter, are we?"

"Not yet," Obi-Wan replied as he navigated the Headhunter back toward Esseles. "Our first stop is Trinkatta Starships to check on our friends. If there's any chance of stopping that other freighter, we'll need all the help we can get!"

CHAPTER TEN

At this point, readers who chose to follow the adventure in the *Star Wars Adventures* Game Book can return to *The Bartokk Assassins.*

On Esseles, the heroes who had been stunned by the Bartokks were fully recovered. Despite Trinkatta's cantankerous nature, he had done a good job of caring for the wounded at his starship factory.

Sitting on a bench in Trinkatta's workshop, Bama Vook gave his son a playful sock in the arm. "I'll bet you're glad to be back on Esseles, eh, son?"

"I'll say!" Chup-Chup declared. "Wait'll I tell my friends about my adventure."

"Perhaps you should delay your storytelling for now," Qui-Gon calmly suggested. "Until we settle the matter of the missing droid starfighters, lives are still in danger. You'll be able to tell your friends soon, I promise."

Qui-Gon turned to Obi-Wan and Leeper. Both the Padawan and the droid were hunkered over a table that was littered with numerous tools. Leeper was examining the Neimoidian prototype hyperdrive engine that had been retrieved from the Bartokk freighter, and Obi-Wan was monitoring a subspace transceiver.

"What do you make of it, Leeper?" Qui-Gon asked.

The droid tapped at the engine. "It's a fast unit, this is," he admitted. "If all those Trade Federation droid starfighters were powered by engines like this, they could be deployed almost anywhere within the next three sectors in a matter of minutes."

"Then I think we can assume that was the Trade Federation's motive for wanting their starfighters built on Esseles," Qui-Gon proclaimed. "If they'd built such threatening weapons within Republic space, they'd be breaking more than a dozen treaties. The Trade Federation representative would be kicked out of the Senate."

"I wouldn't know about that," Leeper admitted. "But I'll tell you this: if that second Bartokk freighter is carrying twenty-five droid starfighters, it can't be for any good reason."

The Jedi Master turned to Obi-Wan and asked, "Any word from Corulag?"

"I sent a message to Corulag Academy," Obi-Wan replied. "They know the Bartokk freighter may be on its way."

"It's a long trip to Corulag," Qui-Gon observed. "It's my guess that the Bartokks plan on delivering the droid starfighters there. If they'd wanted to deploy the starfighters, they could have done so as soon as they left Esseles. If the freighter is traveling below light speed, we'll catch up to it without any problem."

"Actually, we may already have a problem," Obi-Wan admitted. "I tried sending a message to the Jedi chapter house on Rhinnal to check on Adi Gallia's condition. There's no response. I'm only getting static. It might just be subspace interference."

"Then again, there might be trouble on Rhinnal." Qui-Gon grimaced. "We must go to Rhinnal immediately. We'll deal with the Bartokk freighter as soon as we can."

Bama Vook jumped up from his bench. "Leeper and I can take you to Rhinnal in the *Metron Burner.*"

"I'll take you up on that offer, Bama," Qui-Gon said. "Let's get going!"

Nute Gunray paced the main deck of the Trade Federation battleship. He was scheduled to deliver a report to Darth Sidious, and he was not looking forward to it. Still he knew the Sith Lord would not forgive a late communication, so he sat down in front of the holocom.

The image of the cowled Darth Sidious appeared above the transceiver. "What is the report from Esseles?" Darth Sidious demanded.

Nute Gunray struggled to find the best words to answer the question. "There has been an unexpected development," he babbled. "Our two agents have reported they overheard that a Bartokk freighter left Esseles with all fifty droid starfighters and the prototype hyperdrive engine."

"Is that all?" Darth Sidious asked.

Gunray was surprised by the Sith Lord's question. Darth Sidious sounded almost unconcerned about Bartokks. "There is another problem," Gunray added. "Our agents also believe they saw Jedi Knights on Esseles."

"I have little tolerance for *unexpected developments,* Gunray," Darth Sidious responded. "You have not handled this situation well."

"I . . . I will pursue the Bartokk freighter myself!" Gunray boldly stammered.

"Do not bother," Darth Sidious answered. "I have someone else lined up for the job."

The hologram flickered off.

NEXT ADVENTURE:
THE FURY OF DARTH MAUL